THE POND PLAYERS

Linda A. Abbott

Balboa Press books may be ordered through booksellers or by contacting:

Balboa Press
A Division of Hay House
1663 Liberty Drive
Bloomington, IN 47403
www.balboapress.com
1 (877) 407-4847

Because of the dynamic nature of the Internet, any web addresses or
links contained in this book may have changed since publication and
may no longer be valid. The views expressed in this work are solely those
of the author and do not necessarily reflect the views of the publisher,
and the publisher hereby disclaims any responsibility for them.

Any people depicted in stock imagery provided by Getty Images are
models, and such images are being used for illustrative purposes only.
Certain stock imagery © Getty Images.

ISBN: 978-1-9822-4553-5 (sc)
ISBN: 978-1-9822-4552-8 (e)

Library of Congress Control Number: 2020905772

Print information available on the last page.

Balboa Press rev. date: 04/14/2020

BALBOA.PRESS

A DIVISION OF HAY HOUSE

THE POND PLAYERS

In a little pond sits Herman the Fish.

"I am so sad, if I only had a wish…
then I wouldn't have to sit in
this water all day long. I'll cheer
myself up by singing a song!"

He began to sing out loud, and all at once there was a crowd.

They cheered, they laughed,
they clapped, they sang…

And all the sounds through
the small pond rang.

They sang all day.

They played all night, but, without knowing it, they started a fight!

They played so loud, they
sang so strong.

That Otto the Owl didn't
like their song.

"I was sleeping! Can you not see? I
know, you're picking a fight with me!"

"Oh my, oh no, oh dear, oh gee! Please
I don't want you to fight with me!"

"We'll stop all of us. We won't make a sound." And right after that the owl flew down.

He stopped, looked around but they were nowhere to be found. So he began to stroll along the ground.

Asking himself, "How could I be so cruel? I really didn't realize that I was such a fool."

Searching for the creatures, of whom, were so polite. He searched all through the day.

And through the dark of the night.

In the morning he had found those who seemed to be his friends.

For they were caring for poor Otto;
because friendship never ends.

The moral to the story is
one of just a few...

If you are kind to others;
they will be kind to you.

The End.

Printed in the United States
By Bookmasters